FLUBBY

Flubby will Not Take a Bath

To Ann Marie—JEM

PENGUIN WORKSHOP
An imprint of Penguin Random House LLC, New York

First published simultaneously in paperback and hardcover in the United States of America by
Penguin Workshop, an imprint of Penguin Random House LLC, New York, 2021

Visit us online at penguinrandomhouse.com.

Library of Congress Cataloging-in-Publication Data is available.

Manufactured in China

ISBN 9780593382868 (pbk)   10 9 8 7 6 5 4 3 2 1

Flubby will Not Take a Bath

by J. E. Morris

Penguin Workshop

Flubby is dirty.
He needs a bath.

A warm bath will get Flubby
nice and clean.

The bath is ready.

Flubby will not take a bath.

I have shampoo.

It smells nice.

Now Flubby will take a bath.

Flubby will not take a bath.

I have bubbles.

Bubbles are fun.

Now Flubby will take a bath.

Flubby still will not take a bath.

I have a toy fish.

Flubby likes this toy.

Flubby still will not take a bath.

TAP
TAP

Flubby, you are very dirty.
You *must* take a bath!

Baths are fun.

You will see.

Flubby would not take a bath.

But he did take a shower.

BVVVVVV